S0-AJL-918

MYSTERY OF THE
Disappearing
Dogs

by Barbara Brenner

Text illustrations by Blanche Sims

Alfred A. Knopf   New York

This is a Borzoi Book
Published by Alfred A. Knopf, Inc.

Copyright © 1982 by Barbara Brenner
Text illustrations copyright © 1982 by Blanche Sims
Cover illustration copyright © 1982 by Judy Clifford

Library of Congress Cataloging in Publication Data
Brenner, Barbara.
Mystery of the disappearing dogs. (Capers)
Summary: The Garcia twins become detectives in
pursuit of dognappers, fearing that their dog Perro
has become the victim of Operation Hot Dog.
[1. Mystery and detective stories.   2. Dogs—Fiction.
3. City and town life—Fiction   I. Title.   II. Series
PZ7.B7518MX   1982   [Fic]   82-186
ISBN 0-394-95162-X (lib. bdg.)   AACR2
ISBN 0-394-85162-5 (pbk.)

Contents

MYSTERY OF THE
DISAPPEARING DOGS

Prologue

Do you like cities? If you don't, better stop reading right now. Because a city street is where it's all going to happen.

You *know* this street, somehow. Maybe you've been there in real life. Or you've seen it in the movies, or on TV. Imagine. . . .

Brownstone houses, all different colors. Cars parked at curbs, window-box gardens, sidewalks, rows of stone steps. . . .

It's summer. The kids are outside playing ball, or listening to their portable radios, or pitching pennies. Some of the grownups sit on the stoops. Others lean out of windows high above the street to catch an evening breeze. There's a buzz of talk and laughter, a lot of calling back and forth. . . .

"Hey, Freddy, how you been?"

"*Eh, Mario! Como estás?*"

"You going to the movie, Angie?"

You see? It's a typical August evening in a city neighborhood. *So far.*

Now, those two nine-year-old children sitting in front of Number 22—they're the Garcia twins, Elena and Michael. You've already met them if you read a book called *Mystery of the Plumed Serpent.* You'll remember that they live on the second floor of that house with their mother and grandmother. Their father died a long time ago. Their mother works in the office of a lace factory. Grandma stays home and cooks and sews and keeps up with what goes on in the neighborhood. As for Elena and Michael, they are busy with school, and babysitting and playing. One of their favorite games is looking for adventure. Sometimes adventure finds them!

By the way, that's their dog—the little rust and white one with the tail like an ostrich plume. The dog's name is *Perro*. Perro means

dog in Spanish. Now that piece of information
has nothing to do with this story. *But*—Perro
has everything to do with it.

Keep your eye on him. By tomorrow night
this picture will change in one very important
way. And there's one person on the street right
now who knows that.

5

CHAPTER 1
Something Unusual

Elena was speaking softly. That was unusual enough.

"Did you know that you have the most beautiful brown eyes in the world?" she cooed.

She leaned over to hug the bundle of fur sitting at her feet. The bundle of fur looked at her adoringly. It licked her face.

Elena turned to her brother, grinning. *Tease a twin time,* her expression seemed to say. "See," she announced. "Perro licks me. Perro loves me best. I told you so."

Michael grinned. His eyes flashed back at her. *Two can play the teasing game,* they seemed to say.

"Not so, sister dear. Let's examine the facts. Fact one. You just ate a raspberry ice. Fact two.

6

You got it all over your face, as usual. Fact three. Perro licks you on the face. Conclusion: Perro loves raspberry ice the best."

Elena stuck her tongue out at her brother. Her tongue was bright red, evidence for Michael's raspberry ice theory.

"Go soak your head, smart guy," she said mildly.

In a minute they had both forgotten what the teasing was about. And Perro never knew. He ran back and forth between them, his tail like a signal flag wagging the message that he was happy to belong to both of them.

Perro had been in their family six whole months now. Since that famous night when Joe Bowler had come to the house to take Mama to the movies.

Joe had pulled the shivering puppy out from under his sweater.

"And here's a little something for you two," he'd said.

What he never said was where Perro came from. But Elena and Michael had a few ideas about that. Joe Bowler was a customs agent they'd met when they worked on the Plumed Serpent case. Joe did a lot of secret work. Elena and Michael were sure that Perro was connected in some way with Joe's work.

But how? It was fun to try to guess.

Had Perro been in the apartment of a smuggler? A drug dealer? Was he found next to a dead body in a shoot-out?

Even Grandma and Mama played the guessing game. Grandma said she bet Joe Bowler had rescued Perro from a burning warehouse.

Mama said Perro had probably been found on a smuggling ship.

All of these guesses were interesting. So when people asked Elena where she had gotten her dog, she told whichever story came to her head at the moment.

That drove Michael crazy. "Why don't you just stick to the facts?" he'd grumble. (Facts were important to Michael.)

"Because there are no facts to stick to," Elena would reply. (Elena would choose imagination over facts any day.)

And they would drop the subject until the next time.

Right now Michael was saying, "Do you suppose his owner is still looking for Perro?"

"No!" Elena didn't like the idea that Perro had loved and licked someone else in his short life. "You want to know what I really think?" she said to her brother. "I think Joe got him from the dog pound. I think he rescued Perro at the eleventh hour."

Elena loved phrases like "eleventh hour." So scary-sounding. Like a matter of life and death. When she couldn't find adventure in real life, Elena would settle for adventurous words.

"Anyway, he's ours now," said Michael, anxious to change the subject. "And he will be forever, if he behaves himself."

"What do you mean, behaves himself? He's *never* had an accident."

"You know what I mean. Mama and Grandma aren't *muy* happy to have dog hairs all over the red velvet sofa."

"He can't help it if he sheds," Elena said loyally. "Outside of shedding, he's a perfect dog."

"Best on the block," Michael agreed.

"So how many on the block, anyway?" Elena had to know just how many dogs her Perro was competing with.

"I don't know. Five, six, maybe. Here comes Mr. Gold. Let's ask him. He'll know."

Mr. Gold. Imagine him. A small, bent-over old man walking toward them. Picture him in the old gray sweater that he wears winter and summer. Picture the beard that just matches the sweater. Conjure up Mr. Gold clearly, because he is important to the story.

As he came up to them, the twins noted that Mr. Gold was carrying his usual brown paper bag. Michael and Elena knew from experience that it contained a chunk of sweet Turkish halvah wrapped in waxed paper. Mr. Gold was a great source of halvah. He was also a great source of facts, which made him one of Michael's favorite people.

"Mr. Gold, how are you?" asked Michael, for starters.

"How should I be?" Mr. Gold very often answered a question with a question.

Elena had no patience for this chitchat. She cut in with question number three. "Mr. Gold, how many dogs do you think live on our block?"

"Think? I don't think, I know. Seven and a half. The half, that's Rigetti's dog, that toy Boston. You can't count that a whole dog. . . ."

Mr. Gold shook his head in wonder. "Sometimes it seems like we got seventy instead of seven. . . . All that dog dirt in the street. . . . There used to be more, you know. More dogs, I mean. . . ." Mr. Gold seemed to go into a trance, thinking of all the dogs that had lived on the block. And then . . . Mr. Gold stopped walking. He got a very strange expression on his face.

As if he had just thought of something. Something that worried him and made him seem a little older and more bent over. Now he signalled for the twins to come closer. They bent toward him. He whispered a few words, very softly. "Never let your dog off the leash."

How unusual, Michael thought.

"We never do. But why?" he asked.

Mr. Gold's eyes darted up the street, looking for something or someone. But all he said was: "Why? Because I know what I know."

"*What* do you know?" Elena snapped. Elena was not famous for patience.

But the mysterious moment was over.

Mr. Gold changed the subject. Holding out the paper bag, he said in his ordinary voice, "Have a piece of halvah. Go ahead, take. Take the whole thing."

And with that he handed Elena the bag and shuffled off into the dusk.

Michael's eyebrows knit together as he watched Mr. Gold's thin figure disappear. "I wonder what he meant by that. Didn't the way he said it give you the chills?"

Elena shrugged. "He always sounds gloomy and mysterious. Don't pay any attention." She bit into a piece of the sweet candy and handed Michael some.

Elena's probably right, thought Michael, watching her roll the empty candy bag into a ball and stuff it in the back pocket of her yellow jeans.

But Elena was wrong.

They should have paid more attention to Mr. Gold.

CHAPTER 2

It Happens

When they got home that night, the twins told Grandma about meeting Mr. Gold. Grandma went into a long story about how smart Izzy Gold was. "Señor Gold, he is deep," she said, tapping her forehead to show where the deep thoughts of Señor Gold came from.

If Grandma hadn't said that, Michael would have completely forgotten Mr. Gold's strange warning. Even remembering, he couldn't make anything of it. So he tucked the fact away in the back of his head. After all, there's just so much time you can spend on a puzzle unless you find another piece that fits.

In the morning the twins decided to give Perro a bath. Then Elena spent another hour drying his fur with Mama's blow dryer. Perro suffered through it all with good humor, like the sweet dog that he was. When she was finished, Elena called Michael in to see.

"Doesn't he look beautiful?"

"Yeah, great." Michael ran his hand expertly through the fur on Perro's back. "Not a flea on him," he said admiringly. Perro wagged his whole body.

"Ah, good boy, Perro. Give me your paw."

Perro obediently stuck out his paw.

"He remembered!" Michael seemed surprised that all the soap and water hadn't washed the tricks out of Perro's furry head.

Great dog! Clean *and* smart.

And so it was that Michael and Elena decided to go outside and show Perro off in the neighborhood.

They snapped the new orange leash on the new leather collar on the neck of their wonderful, clean, smart, well-behaved dog, Perro.

One four-legged animal and two two-legged ones hurried down the steps of Number 22. None of them suspected that this could be the last time the three of them would go down these steps together.

Elena and Michael passed the leash back and forth between them, taking turns showing off their dog to all their friends. As for Perro himself, he gave his paw politely to everyone. He walked proudly, his tail held high. Everything about him showed that he was a happy dog, proud of his new tricks.

And then came the corner of West Bend Avenue and 94th Street. Afterward Michael and Elena could never remember who had been holding the leash. It didn't matter. What did matter was that a tiny peach-colored poodle suddenly appeared in an apartment house doorway. Alone. The moment Perro saw her, he forgot everything. All the obedience lessons, all the *Sit, Perro! Heel, Perro! Stay, Perro!* All of it went out of his head in a rush of love for the peach-colored poodle.

The little poodle was startled by Perro's sudden, fierce attention. She raced up the street. At that instant, Perro *jerked free of his leash.*

Tail pointed straight out behind him, Perro streaked after the poodle.

The twins took off after Perro.

The superintendent of the apartment house took off after the poodle.

And last, but certainly not least, was the young woman who came dashing out of the apartment building on roller skates. She screamed "Madame Bovary!" and took off after the super and the poodle.

It was a weird group that barreled across Broad Street and raced up along 95th Street toward River Drive. The poodle was still in the lead. But she was no match for the young woman on roller skates. By the time Michael and Elena reached the corner of River Drive and 95th, they could see that the woman had almost caught up with both dogs.

Just then the poodle changed course. She bolted around a corner. Perro bolted after her, with the young woman on roller skates right

17

after Perro, and Michael, Elena and the super
bringing up the rear.

By the time Michael, Elena and the super
rounded the corner the scene had changed
completely. The young woman on roller skates
had the poodle in her arms. She was kissing her

one minute and telling her what a bad dog she had been the next. Elena, who always noticed things, noticed that the woman's hair was exactly the same color as the poodle's. But Michael noticed something more important.

"Where is Perro?"

Perro wasn't there.

Perro had disappeared. Vamoosed. Vanished.

If one of the manhole covers had suddenly opened up and Perro had dropped into it, he couldn't have been more completely gone.

Michael ran up to the strange woman. This was no time for polite talk. "Which way did he go?" he shouted.

"Which way did *who* go?" The woman with the peach-colored hair looked at Michael as if she didn't have the slighest idea what he was talking about.

Elena forgot about hair color.

"Our dog," she wailed.

The woman looked at Elena from under a fringe of false eyelashes. "Oh. That was your dog. I—I don't know," she said vaguely. "I didn't see. I had my eye on Madame Bovary. Ooh, you naughty dog. How could you do that to your momma?"

She turned to the superintendent. "Charlie, you should never have opened that door. I told you always to wait until I have her leash on."

Charlie was puffing so hard that he could hardly talk. He muttered something about the other dog stirring up trouble.

Now the lady on skates looked at her watch. "Oh, no," she groaned. "I'm late for rehearsal. Here," she said, turning to the man she called Charlie, "take Madame Bovary back to the apartment. And don't forget to lock the door."

With that, the lady with the peach hair skated away. Charlie shuffled off in the opposite direction, the poodle tucked under his arm.

Everyone seemed to have forgotten Elena and Michael, and the fact that their dog was missing. "Perro! Here, Perro! Come, Perro!" They ran up and down calling Perro's name.

But the street was empty. The twins looked at each other, dazed. A few minutes ago they had had a dog. And now everything had changed. . . . If only the poodle hadn't come out of the apartment. . . . If only they had held tight to Perro's leash. If only . . . if only. If only they could live those few moments over again. . . .

Michael saw that Elena was about to burst into tears. So was he. He tried to comfort her.

"Listen. Don't worry. He's probably on the way home right now. Someone will pick him up to save him from getting hit by a car. He's got a license on his collar. You'll see, we'll get a call. All we have to do is to go home and . . ."

"Do you really think so?" Elena's eagerness to believe him brought a tight feeling to Michael's throat. *I wish I was sure*, he thought to himself.

"I think we ought to stop at that apartment house first," said Elena as they headed back.

No need to ask which apartment house. Michael knew it was the house of the peach-colored poodle. And no need to ask why. They had to go back to the scene of the crime and try to pick up Perro's trail.

Michael went in alone. He found Charlie

22

and gave him their phone number. "In case you should see or hear anything about Perro," he said. His voice was trembling so much that a tenant who was standing in the lobby came over to see what was wrong.

When Michael came out, the two children hurried toward home, stopping everyone on the way to ask if they had seen a rust-and-white dog.

No one had. The more people they asked, the more Michael's shoulders sagged. The more the corners of Elena's mouth drooped. Was it possible that Perro could disappear into thin air?

"Michael?" Elena thought of something. "Do you think Perro might have met his former owner and recognized him?"

"No, I don't. He wouldn't even remember his former owner. He probably didn't even *have* a former owner."

Elena looked relieved. But her relief didn't last long. Michael had something else on his mind. She could always tell.

"What is it, *hermano*? What are you thinking about?"

"Something that man in the apartment house said."

"You mean Charlie?"

"No. When I went back to give Charlie our phone number, there was a man standing in the lobby. He—he heard us talking and—and—"

"And *what*?" Elena thought she would explode if Michael didn't finish telling her pretty soon.

"He said, 'That's the third one this week.'"

Elena gasped.

"You mean *other* dogs have disappeared?"

"Yes."

"But it's so weird! I mean why . . ."

There was no *why*. There was no *what* or *how*, either.

And still they didn't remember Mr. Gold or his warning.

CHAPTER 3

The Animal Shelter

There were no phone calls waiting for them at home. And when Grandma heard what had happened, she threw her apron over her head. Grandma only threw her apron over her head in times of big trouble.

"*Chiquito Perro, dónde estás?*" she wailed, from under the apron. "Little Perro, where are you?" she asked again in English, in case someone on the other side of the apron didn't understand Spanish. Grandma had forgotten all about dog hairs on red velvet sofas!

Mama came home to find everyone upset. When she heard about Perro's disappearance, she, too, joined the hanky brigade. The tears lasted until long past suppertime.

Elena was the first one to decide that it was time to stop crying and do something.

"Listen," she said to the others. "We have to start getting the word out. Tell everyone on the block that Perro is missing. Offer a reward."

Michael agreed with her. He blew his nose and started a list of things to do.

Things to do about Perro took up almost a whole sheet of paper.

Call the police to see if a dog has been turned in at the station house.

Put an ad in the paper offering a reward for Perro's return.

Talk to Marty and Artie, who drive the police squad-car. Ask them to keep an eye peeled.

"And I think we should go back and see that freaky woman with the poodle," Michael said.

There was a short pause while Elena described the woman on roller skates who had hair the same color as her dog's.

There was another pause when Elena and

Michael realized that they didn't even know the woman's name.

First came the phone call to the police. No luck. Next, a quick trip down the street to see Marty and Artie, who told them to check with the Animal Shelter.

"That's the place where they take stray dogs," the cops told the twins.

By the time they got this information, it was too late to do anything else. Michael and Elena went to bed, worn out from this worst of all bad days.

Next morning was a hard time. Hard to wake up without a tail fanning the air above your face. Hard to start the day without a friendly face wash.

It was Michael who went to pieces this time, and Elena who tried to comfort him. "Never mind, *hermano*," she said tenderly. "We'll find Perro."

As soon as breakfast was over, they left the

house. First stop, the Animal Shelter.

They knew it was the Shelter because it said so. But even if the name hadn't been out front, Elena and Michael would have guessed. The top of the building was covered with sculptures of cats and dogs and birds.

The man at the desk took their names and asked them to wait. The waiting time was filled with *what if's*.

"What if someone took his collar off and kept him?"

"What if he was hit by a car *and* lost his collar and they brought him here dead?"

"What if they've already put him to sleep?" Michael and Elena had heard rumors that dogs were put to sleep at shelters. To sleep *forever*.

It was terrible thinking of that. Luckily, just then a woman in a starched white pantsuit appeared and put an end to the gruesome question-and-answer game. She sat down behind a desk and pulled out a large file box. She had some questions of her own, which she asked in a voice as crisp as her uniform.

"When did you last see the dog? Was he on a leash? Were there any other dogs with him?" She seemed particularly interested in the story of the peach-colored poodle. Michael thought that was a good sign.

Elena could see nothing but bad signs. The worst one was that there seemed to be so many cards in the files of the Animal Shelter. If each one of them represented a missing dog, how could they hope to find Perro?

Elena shared her unhappy thought with Michael when the starchy lady left the room for a minute.

She came back with an announcement. "There is no dog here at the Shelter at this time that fits your description."

At this time stuck in Elena's ears.

Now what does she mean by that? Was there a dog like Perro here at another time? And if so, when? Yesterday? Last year, before Joe brought him to us? This morning?

Elena cleared her throat and with as grown-up a voice as she could manage said, "Could we—uh—look at the dogs? Maybe—maybe you missed him."

The woman shrugged. "Okay, but you'll be sorry," she said, in an almost unfriendly voice.

Michael and Elena followed her down the long corridor. They *were* sorry. It was terrible seeing dogs and cats staring mournfully out of

30

the cages, or barking their anger at being cooped up, or sleeping the sleep of the weak and overtired.

There were big dogs and small dogs, purebreds and mutts. But none of them was Perro.

Finally Elena couldn't stand it. "What happens if no one comes to adopt these animals?"

"Don't ask." Then the volunteer worker in the white suit didn't say anything for a while. When she started to talk again, her voice sounded angry.

"Everyone wants a pet. Then they get it home and the first time it makes on the rug or gets worms they decide it's too much trouble. So back the animal comes to us." She paused, then started a new thought. "Kittens. Puppies. Everyone thinks they're cute. Then when they grow up to be dogs and cats they get rid of them. . . ."

They had come to the end of the corridor. It was clear that Perro wasn't in any of the cages.

"Let's get out of here," said Elena suddenly.

It was too much sadness for one day.

Now that they were about to leave, the volunteer in the white pantsuit became more friendly.

"Listen, if you don't find your dog, come back and I'll pick out a nice puppy for you. I'm here Tuesday and Friday. Ask for Shirley Crimmins."

"What makes you think we won't find our dog?" asked Michael.

"He's wearing a collar with our phone number," Elena added hopefully.

Shirley Crimmins shrugged and her uniform crackled.

"I may as well give it to you straight. Some people don't care how they make money. The collar's the first thing to go. . . . They're willing to sell dogs and cats for . . . all kinds of things."

"Like what?" Michael had to have his facts.

"Just last week we heard of a guy selling cats to a fur dealer. And then there are the creeps who sell dogs to laboratories. And the ones who sell them to dogfight rings for the pit bulls to practice on. I tell you, the schemes people think up. . . ."

Michael and Elena were both pale.

"The latest thing is dogs for ransom. They steal a high-priced pedigree dog and then offer it back to the owner for a price. Or they sell it for big bucks to a kennel or a private person. Some purebreds go for as much as a thousand dollars."

"You mean there are dog kidnappers?"

"That's right. Dognappers. It's a regular business. The latest one around the city calls itself Operation Hot Dog. Bold as brass, they are. But the police will nail them yet," she added grimly.

Elena thought she had found a silver lining to this very black cloud. "Dognappers wouldn't take Perro, then. He's just a mutt," she said.

The silver lining didn't hold up for very long.

"Honey, you'd be lucky if they took him for ransom. It's better than a laboratory or the dogfight gang."

Now they were back in the entrance lobby.

It was a good thing, too, because Michael and Elena couldn't bear much more. They said good-bye to the starchy Ms. Crimmins and started down the steps of the Shelter.

They had learned a lot this morning. But it wasn't an easy lesson. Still, they had to sort it all out and see what the next step would be in their search for Perro.

"You can't trust anybody," said Michael bitterly. "If there is a dognapping ring, anyone could be in it. Even that woman on roller skates. In fact, the more I think of it the more I believe she *is*."

"She probably uses the poodle as a decoy," added Elena.

"On the other hand," Michael said, "it could be the super. Maybe he let the poodle out on purpose."

"Oh, Michael," said Elena. "Next thing you'll be suspecting Mr. Gold."

Mr. Gold. *Finally*. As soon as they remembered him, they remembered what he had said.

"Mr. Gold knows something," said Elena grimly. "We've got to talk to him right away. As soon as we phone in the ad."

But as it turned out there was someone else they had to see first.

CHAPTER 4

Meet
Bonnie Balsam

When they got home, an excited Grandma told them that *la Señora* had called. It took them a few minutes to figure out Grandma's speedy Spanish. But when they did, they realized that *la Señora* was the woman with the poodle. Her name was Bonnie Balsam and she wanted to see them right away. Maybe she had seen Perro!

They raced back downstairs and through the streets to the apartment house on West Bend Avenue. On the way they reviewed their list of clues, or facts, as Michael called them.

"Number one is what the man in that apartment house said—dogs are disappearing from this neighborhood.

"Number two is what the lady at the Shelter said—there's a ring of dognappers operating in this area!

"Number three is what Mr. Gold told us. We've got to go see him as soon as we finish here. Find out what he knows.

"And there's one more thing," Michael added soberly. "This woman we're going to see—the one with the peach-colored hair—I've seen her somewhere before."

Elena scoffed. "Seen her? Where? At the library? In the supermarket? Listen," she added, giggling a little, "if you saw her skating down the frozen-food aisle, you'd remember it!"

"She's fact number four," said Michael.

"Three-and-a-half," said Elena.

Just then they arrived at the scene of the crime.

Charlie the super didn't seem too happy to see them.

"Here they are," he said nastily. "The ones who started all the trouble."

Was the super trying to cover for himself by blaming them?

"Well, the nerve of him," Elena fretted, and would have had more to say if Michael hadn't squeezed her arm.

"Never mind," he whispered to her. He spoke to Charlie in a friendly tone.

"Say, Bonnie Balsam asked to see us. By the way, where have I heard that name before?"

The super gave Michael one of those boy-are-you-dumb looks. "Mean to tell me you don't know who Bonnie Balsam is?"

So who's Bonnie Balsam? And why does she roller skate and wear glittery pants? And why does she have the same color hair as her poodle? And why do I think I've seen her before?

Before Michael had a chance to ask any of these questions, Charlie supplied the answers.

"She's a rock star," he said proudly. "Roller disco rock. It's the newest thing. Belongs to a group — The Holy Rollers. You musta heard of them."

"I'm not sure. Where do they perform?" Michael wanted to know.

"Well, right now they're between engagements. But they were singing in that disco down the street for a while."

"You mean Daffy's?" said Michael excitedly. "That's it. I saw her picture out front on the window."

So. Bonnie Balsam was a rock star, eh. The big question now was whether the rock star was putting on an act!

"Guess you heard what happened last night," the super said.

"No. What happened?"

"Her dog. The little poodle. She's walking it, someone comes up behind her and—grabs it."

So. Another dog disappearance! That's why she called.

"That's when she asked me if I knew how to reach you. She's waiting for you," Charlie said. "You can go up yourselves. It's 15–c."

He pointed the twins toward the elevator.

Any other time, Michael and Elena would have enjoyed that elevator. They would have loved the fancy doors with their shiny brass handles, the old-fashioned rosebud-carved ceiling and the murals that decorated the walls.

But today wasn't the day for enjoyment. They had other things on their minds.

For one thing, Elena recycled some of her previous ideas about Bonnie Balsam. She couldn't be in with dognappers. She wouldn't kidnap her own dog!

The elevator stopped and they got out.

They rang the doorbell of 15–C and waited.

It was quite a while before the peephole opened. They heard a lock being unlocked, and then the door swung open.

There was Bonnie Balsam. Or was it? This woman wore no makeup, no glittery pants, no skates. Her hair was black and short and straight. She was wearing shorts and a sweatshirt that said The Holy Rollers. She looked like she had been crying.

"Come in," she said wearily. "We gotta talk."

"What happened to your hair?" Elena blushed. She hadn't been able to hold back the question.

"That fuzzy one is a wig." Bonne Balsam allowed herself a weak smile. "I had it made to match Madame Bovary's fur. It was just a goof." Her eyes filled with tears. "Bummer," she said. "Guess you heard about last night."

41

"The super told us." Elena said, already feeling sorry for Bonnie.

"I was wondering if you found out anything. I'm real sorry I didn't pay more attention when your dog was—er—disappeared. Guess I didn't think about how I'd feel. Well," Bonnie Balsam sighed. "Now I know."

She told them what had happened to her. "They came up behind me, dropped something over my head and snatched the dog leash out of my hand. I could hear Madame Bovary howling. One of them whispered, 'Don't call the cops or your dog is dead.' " She shuddered. "By the time I got the sack off my head they were gone."

Elena gasped. "We've already told the police about Perro. Does that mean they'll kill him?"

"Hold it," Michael told Elena gently. "Let's hear all the facts first." He turned to Bonnie. "Don't you remember anything else?" he asked.

"N-no, not a thing."

They told Bonnie Balsam their list of clues.

It sounded pretty puny even to them. But Bonnie was polite, and she listened even when Elena, in a burst of honesty, told her that they had placed Bonnie Balsam on the suspect list for a while.

When they were finished, Bonnie Balsam sighed and pulled a scented pink tissue from a fancy silver-colored box.

She blew her nose loudly and sighed again.

"I figure sooner or later those bums are going to be in touch with us. But I can't stand the waiting. So I have an idea. Why don't we each put an ad in the paper? Offer a reward. Make it high enough to bring the rats out of their holes."

Elena and Michael exchanged looks. They had already thought of that. But where would they get enough money to attract the kind of rats who steal dogs for ransom? Bonnie Balsam seemed to understand the looks.

"Hey, never mind about the money," she said. "The Holy Rollers have made a record. It's only a 45, but it's bringing in the bucks.

I'm loaded, temporarily, so I'll take care of your part of the reward. After all, we're in this together now." She sat down and wrote out a check and handed it to them.

It was made out to Elena and Michael Garcia. And it was for five hundred dollars! Just like that. As Elena and Michael stammered out their thanks, the tears started up again.

Bonnie Balsam seemed embarrassed. "Hey, you can pay me back some day." She changed the subject.

"Listen, I have an appointment now. I have to go. Keep in touch. Here," she offered gently, "take these with you." She handed the silver-colored box of tissues to Elena.

Elena and Michael thanked her and left. They were waiting for the elevator when Bonnie opened her door and called to them again.

"Hey, wait a sec."

She wants her tissues back, thought Elena. *She wants her check back,* thought Michael. But in fact, Bonnie Balsam didn't want anything back. She wanted to give them something. Information.

"I just thought of something," she said when the twins were back inside. "That day your dog disappeared—just before I didn't see him anymore, I saw a red van pulling away from the curb. I didn't think anything of it at the time. . . . And then last night, after, y'know, I got the sack off my head, I think I saw the same van. And I just now put it together."

Fact number four!

CHAPTER 5

Hector

Michael said, "Let's stop at Mr. Gold's house on the way home. Let's find out what he knows. See if he knows anything about a red van. Pay attention to whether he looks a certain way when I ask him."

Elena agreed to keep her eyes peeled.

Mr. Gold was sitting on the steps outside, as usual. As usual, he was wearing his gray sweater and a gloomy expression.

"I heard about your dog," he told them. "It's a terrible thing," he added in a sad voice.

They filled Mr. Gold in on the details. Michael told him about Perro, about the poodle and Bonnie Balsam, even about the man in the lobby, and what he had said. And last, but not least, he told Mr. Gold about the red van.

Elena watched carefully to see if Mr. Gold's face changed when they mentioned the van. It didn't. Not one bit. And that *was* suspicious. Why was his expression so carefully the same? Why did his hands shake a little as he plucked at his beard? Was it because Mr. Gold was old and a little trembly? Or was he afraid of something? Or someone?

When Michael finished his story, Mr. Gold sighed sadly.

"Such a calamity! Not that it surprises me. Why should I be surprised?"

"Why shouldn't you be surprised, Mr. Gold?" Michael shot the question at him. "Did you know it was going to happen? If you did, you should have warned us!"

Mr. Gold walked right into Michael's trap. "Well, I tried. . . . I said . . ." His voice trailed off as he realized he was getting in deeper and deeper.

"Listen, what do I know? Nothing," he answered himself.

There was a funny silence. It reminded

47

Elena of the end of a TV show when they freeze the action. No one moved. No one said anything. The whole street seemed to be frozen, listening.

Michael wasn't about to give up now. "You mean you don't know anything about a dognapping ring or a red van? Nothing at all?"

Silence.

Elena tried it her way. "Please, Mr. Gold, Perro is the only dog we ever had. We love him so much."

Mr. Gold fixed his pale eyes on Elena. His face softened. He paused, then said in a low voice, "Believe me, I don't know from any dark red van with *Jersey plates.*"

The twins gasped. But before they could ask about this new clue, Mr. Gold gave them another. This time it was hardly more than a twitch of his lips. It could almost have been a sigh, or a breeze blowing through the one tree on the block. But Elena heard it. What Mr. Gold said was, "Talk to Hector."

Talk to Hector? Hector who?

Mr. Gold stood up, picked up the newspaper he had been sitting on, and went inside.

Period. End of interview. *Finito.*

"Are you sure he said Hector?" Michael was worried that they might have gotten the name wrong.

"That's what he said. I'm positive," Elena insisted.

There were probably fifteen Hectors in the neighborhood. Maybe even twenty. How were they ever going to know which one they should talk to?

Time was wasting. Elena and Michael went home and told Grandma about the latest developments. They gave her the check, which she put in a safe place under the flan pan on a high shelf. Then the three of them started their Hector list. It grew longer and longer. They could see that they would run out of paper and patience before they ran out of Hectors.

"This is so dumb," Elena fumed. "I wish we

could *make* Mr. Gold tell us. Why wouldn't he tell? Maybe he's in on it. Maybe he's a member of the gang."

"Now, *niña*," Grandma said soothingly. "You must understand Señor Gold. He is like a wise old owl. He watches and he learns but he does not speak. Because if he does, the street will not trust his presence. Everyone will become silent as a stone. Also, if Izzy Gold isn't telling you everything, is because he's *muy* scared, no? You know how it is with the bad ones. If someone gives away their secrets they are angry and could take revenge. Señor Gold is full of fear, but he tells us a name. It is up to us to figure out who it is."

"That'll take a month. By that time Perro could be dead." Elena's voice was getting shaky again.

"Don't say that!" Michael couldn't stand it when Elena talked about Perro being dead. But he had to admit things didn't look rosy. It had been more than a day since Perro's disappearance. So far, they had only a few clues. In fact,

50

as Elena pointed out bitterly, they were worse off than they were yesterday at this time. Now another dog was missing. And they didn't dare go back to the police or even call Joe Bowler for help. *No cops*, the dognappers had warned. *Nowhere* was where they were.

It was at this point that Grandma's window came to the rescue. It gave everyone a new *view* of the situation, you might say.

As Grandma looked out of it, she saw one of the neighbors. "There goes Maria Santiago," Grandma said. "Poor thing. Look how old she looks. That boy of hers, he's making her old. Driving her crazy, that bum. They say he's out of jail again and back on the street. Such a no-good, that one. If I had a boy like Hector Santiago, I'd . . ."

Hector. The name rang out in the room.

Hector Santiago. Of course. *That* Hector.

"Boy, are we dumb!" Michael yelled. "The one Hector we didn't think of!"

They were so happy to have solved one mystery that for a minute they forgot that it was only one little piece of a bigger one. That bigger one might even be Operation Hot Dog.

Everyone talked at once.

"Can we be sure?"

"What do we do now?"

"Be careful of that one!"

Elena and Michael spent the next few hours making plans to talk to Hector. They worked out every detail until they were all letter perfect.

The next step was to find Hector. How? The best way was through word-of-mouth on the street. The street would get word to Hector.

So that evening Michael and Elena went into the street. . . . They met a lot of people. Wherever they went, they mentioned Hector Santiago. Where could they find him? They wanted to talk to him. They had a business deal for him. They left it to the street to deliver the message. And it did.

Sometime during the night, someone left a note under their door. It said, "Alcort Hotel, noon." It wasn't signed, but it didn't have to be. They knew who it was from.

At fifteen minutes to twelve the next day, the twins were already in front of the Alcort, a block from their house. They paced nervously up and down, wondering if it was too soon to go in.

"We don't want to blow the set-up," said Elena, who had heard that expression on TV.

"Let's synchronize our watches," said Michael, who watched a bit of TV himself.

At one minute to noon, Elena hissed "Zero hour," and they went in.

The Alcort Hotel was dirty. Dirty green carpet. Dirty lobby. Even a dirty desk clerk. It was a perfect place for thieves and muggers and dope dealers, Elena and Michael decided. Anything could happen at the Alcort.

Which of the shady characters sprawled in the lobby was Hector Santiago, they wondered. They didn't have to wonder long.

Suddenly a voice behind them said, "You wanted to see Hector? So here he is."

What a voice. So rasping. Like a saw going

through wood. It set Elena's teeth on edge. She and Michael turned at the same instant and were face to face with Hector Santiago.

He was not a pleasant sight. Greasy hair, dirty pants, a shirt with the sleeves cut out and a hideous tattoo of a spider on one arm. That was Hector. And to top it off, when he grinned, as he was doing now, there was a big space

where Hector's front teeth should have been. Hector was *gross*.

Being this close to Hector seemed to do something to Michael's voice. He opened his mouth but no words came out.

"Whatsa matter, cat got your tongue?" Hector jeered. Elena could see that Michael wasn't going to start this little talk. So she did.

"Do you happen to know where our dog Perro might be? He's disappeared." Elena felt a little like a dog herself—like a little puppy whining up at a wolf.

"Ah! So it's dog business, is it? How is it you come to Hector Santiago?"

Elena knew that whatever happened, they mustn't mention Mr. Gold.

So she shrugged and said, just as she and Michael had rehearsed it, "We just thought you might know. You know what's goin' down on the street. We're willing to pay."

Hector threw back his head and laughed.

"You kids don't have enough dough to interest Hector Santiago." Elena wondered why

Hector always talked about himself as if he was talking about another person.

By this time Michael had found his voice.

"Don't be so sure, Hector," he said smoothly. And he told Hector about the other dog, about Bonnie Balsam and about the five hundred dollars for each dog. "And no questions asked," Michael added.

Hector wasn't laughing anymore. He was dead serious.

"A thousand bucks. Now that's more like it. That Hector might be interested in. But he can only give information. He don't deliver goods."

"No," said Michael firmly. "You have to get the dogs back, otherwise it's no deal."

"Hey, kid, be cool. Don't tell Hector how to do it, okay?" Hector's eyes narrowed.

He's thinking it over, thought Elena. *It's just as we figured. The next thing he'll do is ask to meet Bonnie Balsam.*

Sure enough. Hector pulled a card out of his pocket.

"Go to this place for dinner tonight. Be

there by seven. Bring the dame with you. Five
hundred bucks in cash for the information.
Then when you get your dogs back five hundred more. That's the deal. And don't tell nobody, if you want to see those dogs again."

Hector Santiago turned around and walked
across the dirty green carpet to the door.

CHAPTER 6
Taza de Oro

Taza de Oro. That's what it said on the card that Hector had given them.

"What does Cuban-Chinese *cuisine* mean?"

"It means cooking. And the *Taza de Oro* means cup of gold," Michael informed Elena.

"I know that part. Anyway, I don't see what a *restaurant* has to do with getting Perro back."

Neither did Michael. But they wasted no time getting in touch with Bonnie and reporting what Hector Santiago had said.

Bonnie agreed that they would have to meet him. "I'm nervous," she confessed, chewing one of her purple fingernails. "Maybe we *should* tell someone. I mean, just in case."

"He said, 'Don't tell nobody.' " Elena did a

perfect imitation of Hector's raspy voice. "We can't take a chance."

There were so many things to worry about, it was hard for the twins to know where to begin. At least, Bonnie had told them that she would take care of supplying the five hundred dollars in cash.

But the biggest worry was what to tell Grandma and Mama. They would surely ask where the twins were going at suppertime.

Elena could almost *hear* Grandma saying, "A *restaurant*? You are going to eat there? You don't like my *pollo frito* anymore?" Mama would be puzzled and insulted, too. But they couldn't tell anyone what their real mission was—otherwise the deal would be off, according to Hector.

The story they finally told was that Bonnie was treating them to supper so that they could talk about a plan to get the dogs back. It was not exactly a lie, but still they worried. Especially Michael. Michael seemed to have a whole Chinese menu of things to worry about.

59

He went back and forth from Column A to Column B.

"And I'll tell you another thing about Hector," said Michael, frowning. "What he's doing makes him a *snitch*. If he takes our money without telling the gang, that gang is gonna be out to get him. I wouldn't want to be around when that happens. They might even come to the restaurant."

Michael worried all afternoon. When they went to pick up Bonnie that evening, he was still worrying. Elena couldn't stand it.

"Tell you what," she said to Michael. "Why doesn't Bonnie go in with *one* of us. The other person will stay outside and keep an eye peeled."

"Good idea," said Michael. "You can stay outside."

"The heck I will! Just because I'm a girl you think you can stick me with the dull part. *You* stay outside."

The outside-inside argument got louder and louder. Finally Bonnie said, "Hey, slow down a minute, you two. How about tossing a coin?"

They tossed. Elena lost. She sulked. "I won't be in on the action. I won't even get any egg rolls."

"I'll bring you a doggie bag," Michael said soothingly, and he was immediately sorry he'd said it. Any mention of dogs made all three of them sad.

"Let's get going." Bonnie was strapping on her skates, her lips pressed into a thin line. "We'll see what the little punk has to say."

As they headed toward the *Taza de Oro*, the same question was in everyone's mind. What was to keep Hector Santiago from giving them useless information for their money? How could they double check what Hector said? Worse still, how did they know he wouldn't bring someone with him, hold them up and simply take the money?

"Well," said Bonnie out loud, "first he'll have to find it. And it's not in my handbag. That dumb I'm not."

"Where did you put it?"

"You'll never guess," Bonnie shouted over her shoulder, as she zigzagged her way through the crowds on Broad Street. "And he won't either." She twirled and came to a quick stop in front of the restaurant.

"This is where we leave you," Michael told Elena.

"Yeah, yeah, I know."

Elena looked around. "See that coffee shop across the street? I'll sit over there. That way I can watch the restaurant. If I see anything at all that's suspicious, I'll call Joe Bowler."

"You be careful," Michael said.

"Be careful yourself, Michael. And don't forget my egg rolls."

Elena crossed the street. Michael and Bonnie Balsam entered the *Taza de Oro*.

Bonnie had skated to a booth and was seated before anyone could say "no skates allowed." Michael sat down next to her. They both looked around.

The *Taza de Oro* was an odd place. The decorations weren't Cuban and they weren't Chi-

nese. In fact, there was nothing about the place that you'd remember. That may have been why Hector had picked it in the first place.

Michael and Bonnie weren't very hungry. But Hector's orders were to have dinner. "Let's order before he comes," said Bonnie. "I know when I meet him I'll completely lose my appetite."

They ordered spareribs and egg rolls and some fried green bananas. When the food came it smelled good, but Michael couldn't bring himself to eat. He felt guilty about Elena already.

Bonnie looked over at him. "Hey, kid," she said. "Relax."

"I wish he'd come," Michael said nervously.

"Not eating won't make him come any quicker."

They finished the egg rolls and still Hector hadn't shown. *Where the heck was Hector?*

To take his mind off the subject, Michael picked up a menu. He made believe he was ordering something for Elena. Would she like Cuban shredded beef with fried bananas? Or would she rather have sweet and sour pork?

He never did decide. Because just then a voice said, "Do you mind if Hector joins the party?"

At that moment, Michael decided that if slime had a sound, it would be Hector Santiago's voice.

Hector hung his jeans jacket on a hook above the booth and sat down. He helped him self to a sparerib and dipped it in duck sauce. "You the dame with the poodle? You got the money with you?" he asked Bonnie, not waiting for an answer to his first question.

"I have the money. You all set to give us the information?" Bonnie sounded almost as tough as Hector.

"Take it easy. All in good time." Hector helped himself to a piece of fried banana.

"Where ya gah the money?" Hector asked, with his mouth full. "You ga it—in your hanbag?"

"Never mind where I have it. *You* have exactly two minutes to tell us about the dogs. After that, the deal is off. I take my dough and go elsewhere."

"Hey, hey, slow down. Hector'll tell you. He'll tell you. Be cool."

Michael watched Hector wipe his greasy hands on his pants.

"It's like . . . very delicate. Very secret. You understand, Hector isn't part of this Hot Dog operation. Like, he just has contacts. . . ."

Anyone could tell that Hector was lying about Hector and about his connections with Operation Hot Dog.

"Do you want a description of the dogs?"

"Naw." Hector looked up at the ceiling as if Madame Bovary's picture was there. "Small apricot toy poodle, weighs 10–12 pounds, very rare color, valuable because it's used on record covers. Right?"

He was grinning as if he had just gotten an A on a test.

"How—how do you know all that?" Bonnie was pale.

It was clear that the dognappers had Madame Bovary.

Michael couldn't wait any longer. He interrupted, "What about Perro? Small rust-and-white mixed breed. You've seen him, haven't you?"

Hector brushed Michael's question aside. "One dog at a time," he growled. "Now let's see," he continued, "the poodle is scheduled to be sold soon. So we have to make our deal quickly."

What did Hector mean by sold? And why was he avoiding the subject of Perro?

Bonnie Balsam was picking at the purple polish on ner nails. She didn't look up.

"Give it to me straight," she said. "If I don't pay you, what will happen to my dog?"

"If we can't make some bucks on her fancy looks she'll go down to a man in North Carolina who deals in dog fights. He'll buy her for the pit bulls to practice on."

Hector seemed to enjoy making Bonnie Balsam turn pale. Michael thought he would enjoy punching Hector.

"Okay," said Bonnie quietly. "You win. I'll do whatever you say."

"Now that's more like it. You hand over the dough, you get an address. You wait twenty-four hours. Then you can go there and pick up your mutt."

"But what about . . ." Michael started to protest.

"And you, kid." He turned to Michael as if he suddenly remembered him again. "Don't you get wise!"

Bonnie looked at Michael. What could they do? They had to give Hector half the money. Bonnie started to reach down to undo her skate.

Hector was facing the front of the restaurant. He gazed casually out the plate glass window, as if whatever Bonnie Balsam was fishing for in her shoe skates had nothing to do with him.

Suddenly Hector jumped up from the table as if he'd seen a ghost. "I'll be right back. Gotta go to the can," he muttered, and disappeared through the door marked Gentlemen.

Michael and Bonnie drank their tea and waited for Hector to come back. The waiter came and cleared the table and brought more tea. Still Hector had not returned.

Finally Michael said, "I'm going in to see what's keeping him."

He could almost have guessed what he would find. No Hector. Hector had gone out the window of the Gentlemen's room. Hector was no gentleman.

"Now what do you suppose made him take off like that?" Michael wondered as he slumped down in the booth with Bonnie.

"He must have seen someone he was mighty scared of." Bonnie looked beaten. "So here I sit, with a skate full of money. And no information." She picked up the check and slid out of the booth. "Let's go," she said, sadly. "Elena must be worried. We've been in this place a long time."

Michael slid out of his side of the booth. He never noticed that something was still hanging on the hook by their booth.

Hector had left his jacket.

CHAPTER 7

The Coffee Shop

Elena had been waiting in the coffee shop drinking a Coke. And sulking. *It's not fair that Michael wins the best assignment. He'll know where Perro is before I will. And he'll be in on all the excitement.*

She finished her Coke and ordered another one. While she waited, she wriggled nervously and twisted around on the stool. But one thing Elena didn't do. She didn't take her eyes from the front of the building across the street. Watching the *Taza de Oro* was her assignment. And even though it wasn't so exciting, she knew how important it was.

Elena had been at her post about ten minutes when Hector Santiago came slouching up the street. She saw that he was alone. That was

70

good. She also saw that no one was following him. That was good, too.

Elena fingered the dimes in her pocket. They were there in case she had to call someone in a hurry. Like Joe Bowler. Joe Bowler had a private number you could call night or day. 693-7895. She knew it by heart.

Now Hector was standing outside the *Taza de Oro* looking in. Reading the menu, maybe. Or checking to see if Michael and Bonnie had obeyed his orders. At last he pushed open the door. With her eyes on the restaurant, Elena let her imagination go to work. She imagined Hector looking around inside with that slit-eyed sneaky look of his. She imagined him seeing Michael and Bonnie. Now he would be sliding into the booth with them. In her mind's eye she saw them getting down to business. She could almost hear Hector's buzz-saw voice spelling out the deal.

Another fifteen minutes went by. *What was taking them so long?*

"You want something else?" That was the waitress's way of telling Elena that she couldn't take up a seat without ordering.

"Er—yes. I'll have a burger, please."

More time. The burger came.

Elena nibbled at it. Not very good. Elena tried to imagine that the hamburger was an egg roll. This time her imagination failed her.

What is going on in there? What if there has been an ambush? A robbery? A shootout? Bonnie and Michael could be dead, for all I know. And I'm sitting out here in this crummy coffee shop eating a crummy hamburger.

Just then Elena noticed a police car pull up in front of the coffee shop. *Marty and Artie! How come they were here?* Her throat closed up with fear. They must have gotten a call. Something had happened in the restaurant. She gulped, swallowed and almost choked on a piece of pickle. By the time she stopped coughing, Marty and Artie were pushing open the door to the coffee shop.

Elena put some change on the table for the waitress and picked up her check. She wiped her mouth and slid off the stool. Moving toward them, she expected to hear *"Elena, we've been looking all over for you. Don't worry, we have the whole place staked out. We know all about the dognapping and the ransom. We'll get them."*

73

But that conversation only took place in Elena's head. Marty and Artie had headed straight for the takeout counter. They were ordering burgers and coffee to go!

She moved toward them. "Hi, Marty. Hi, Artie." Her voice shook a little.

Elena had a new decision to make. On the one hand, here were two cops, right *next* to her. She could tell them the whole story and get their help. What a relief that would be. *Now*, she was thinking. *Do it now.*

"Hey, Elena." They both smiled at her.

On the other hand—she wasn't supposed to tell anyone. Telling might ruin everything. Hector had said that if they told, the dogs would be killed. Hector Santiago was so bad. But still. . . .

Marty and Artie had gotten their order. They were moving toward the door. "See ya 'round, Elena," Marty said casually. *Now*. Last chance!

Too late. Marty and Artie were out the door and getting into the patrol car.

Two minutes after they drove away, Elena spotted a dark red van with Jersey plates pulling into a metered parking space on the side street next to the coffee shop!

A man in dark glasses and a tough-looking blonde woman got out of the van. They sauntered across the street to the *Taza de Oro*. They seemed to be reading the menu in the window, just as Hector had done. That, thought Elena, must be a pretty interesting menu.

New facts require new thinking, Michael would have said. Elena went over all the facts she could think of. One. There was a dark red van with Jersey license plates that had been at the scene of the crime. Two. Hector Santiago appeared to be connected to the crime. And now—three. It looked very much like there was a connection between Hector and the red van.

The menu readers had their backs to the coffee shop. And to the van. And to Elena. Elena was sure they were really looking in the window of the *Taza de Oro* for Hector. In fact, she wondered why they weren't seeing him. She herself had seen him go in. What goes in must come out, *verdad*?

Should she look inside the red van before they came back? Maybe the inside would offer some answers. Luckily, the van was parked so that the front faced Broad Street. The back faced the side street. Elena could look into the back of the van without being seen from across the street.

She got up and paid her check. She got her change. Her heart was hammering. She walked out the door and around the corner. Slow down, Elena, she told herself.

She walked a few steps past the van and then came back. She stood at the curb, a few inches from the back door of the van.

Any minute they may come back.

The glass panels at the back of the van were just a little too high for her. Darn.

She tried standing on her toes, but she still couldn't see. She climbed up onto the back bumper and looked inside. It was dark, but the street light reflected off something metal inside. Animal cages? She had to find out.

Elena got down. She put her hand on the door handle. She tried to look as if every day she opened dark red vans and looked inside. Any second she expected to hear, *Hey, what do you think you're doing?*

She pulled down on the handle. Double darn. Is it locked?

One more time. She winced at the noise as the door swung open. Quickly, she climbed inside and pulled the door closed behind her.

The first thing Elena noticed was the smell. That furry, funky, unmistakable smell of animals.

At the same time she noticed the cages. Two large ones made of metal. There was no mistaking what they were. They were the kind of cages used to transport dogs.

Elena's heart was beating fast. She was already rehearsing what she would tell Michael. *I have hard evidence that they are using the dark red van to transport dogs.*

She looked out through the windshield of the van. The man and woman were still standing in front of the restaurant. She was sure now that they were keeping an eye on Hector.

If she could just find something more than a *smell* of dog before she left the van. Maybe under those blankets in the corner.

Elena started rummaging through the blankets. She didn't know what she was looking for. But whatever it was, she had to find it fast! This must be *van*-dalism, she thought, giggling the way you do sometimes when there's nothing to laugh about.

At that precise moment the front door of the van opened. No more time for giggling. No time to get out of the van. No *way* to get out of the van. As soon as Elena heard the sound she ducked under the smelly dog blankets.

She heard a strange voice ask, "Where the — were you?"

Then she recognized Hector's voice answering, "I saw these two cops in a squad car and I thought they were staking out the joint, so I split. I went out the back way and waited awhile until I saw the coast was clear."

Then there was a woman's voice, "You sitting back there or up front with us?"

Elena held her breath. But before Hector

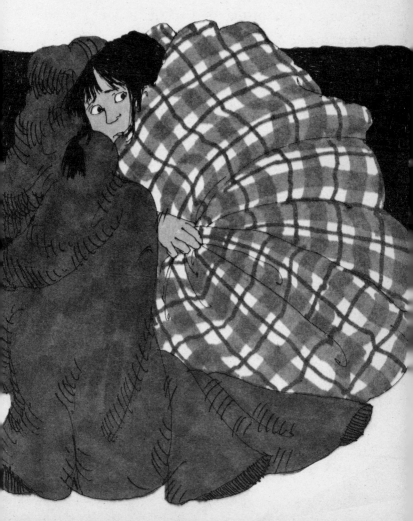

could answer, the woman asked another question. "You get the money?"

Elena strained to hear the answers to both of these important questions. But she couldn't hear a thing. All she could do was wait, knowing that if Hector decided to sit in back, she'd be discovered.

But he must have decided to sit up front. She heard the front doors slam.

In a minute, she felt the van moving. Moving where?

CHAPTER 8
Across the Bridge

I have to be clever. Even though I am scared half out of my wits, I must try to stay calm.

Elena knew that if they discovered her, she would be in big trouble. But there was no sense dwelling on that. First she had to somehow figure out where they were going.

It was a little like playing blindman's buff, this riding in the back of a van. Her ears told her they were on a highway. They'd been on it about—she could barely see her watch—fifteen minutes. Now the van was slowing up. There was a clinking sound. What was that? She'd heard that sound before. *Oh, I know. Money being dropped into an automatic toll machine. Yes.* Now there was that funny noise tires make on metal. They must be going over a bridge. Then, more highway.

Elena was getting sleepy. There was hardly any air in the back of the van. She fought to keep her eyes open. Let's see. It's about twenty-five minutes since the bridge. Now they were slowing down. What? Another bridge? She tried hard to think of the map of the city. Where did you cross two bridges, one after the other?

The sound of the tire treads was different now. Slower. Softer. They must have turned off onto a blacktop road. Four more minutes and the van stopped.

Elena huddled further down under the dog blankets. If she could have made herself invisible she would have.

Now they will open the back and discover me.

She practiced what she would say. *Listen, I don't know anything and if I did, I wouldn't talk.*

But they wouldn't believe her. They would

kill her, probably. Maybe torture her first.

Elena's imagination ran on. Meanwhile, the three people up front got out and slammed the doors of the van. Elena heard with relief the sound of their shoes crunching on something soft as they walked away. So, for the moment at least, she was safe. Alive and well in a dark red van somewhere two bridges away from the city.

Elena sat up. She fished around in her pocket and found one of Bonnie Balsam's pink scented tissues. She blew the itchiness of dog hairs out of her nose and had a short talk with herself.

Well, are you going to sit here all day? Or are you going to investigate? What would Michael do? She knew the answer. Michael would certainly investigate if he were here now.

Suddenly Elena missed Michael. She would have given anything to have him here now. Two bridges away seemed much too far for one twin to be from another. *Try not to think about it,* she told herself.

Carefully, Elena opened the back of the van

a crack. It creaked slightly and sent shivers up her spine. She put her eye to the space and looked out. No one in sight.

The van seemed to be parked at the end of a blacktop driveway. In the fading light Elena was able to see a house and garage at the end of the driveway. Beyond the two buildings she glimpsed a sandy slope that led to a beach of some kind. She sniffed the salty air.

"Why, I'm at a seashore!" she said out loud.

She opened the door a little wider. Just then lights went on in the house. Now Elena could see that it was an old house, weather-beaten and ramshackle. The garage was even more dilapidated. It didn't even have doors.

Time to make a move. Once more Elena checked to see if the coast was clear. Then she opened the van door, slid out, closed the door as quietly as she could and raced toward the garage.

She decided to begin her investigation there. Luckily, the first thing she found was a flashlight that worked.

The second thing was a burlap sack. The sack stood in the corner and it was certainly full of something.

Elena hesitated to open it. Who knows what could be in a burlap sack in a dilapidated and spooky-looking garage?

Carefully she untied the top of the sack and shined the flashlight into the opening. As soon as she did it, she almost wished she hadn't. The sack was filled to the brim with dog collars!

When Elena realized what they were, she emptied the whole sack out onto the garage floor. All the collars spilled out—blue ones and orange ones and red ones and plain leather ones and even collars studded with fake sequins and diamonds. Many of them had names of dogs on them—ALFIE, PRINCE, BÉBÉ, SIR LAWRENCE, SNOOPY. There were license tags. And vaccination tags. All there. All except a tag that said *Perro*.

Elena went through them all again. That was when she found the little silver collar with a tag that said *Madame Bovary*.

So! Here was clear proof. They had Madame Bovary. Or at least she had been here.

It was time to find a phone. Time to call Joe's private number and describe where she was. Time to lead the rescue squad to the scene of the crime, using all she remembered from the ride in the van.

Elena might have been able to beam her rescuers to where she was. But she never had a chance to try.

As she put the flashlight back on the shelf, a voice said, "All right, freeze!"

It was the voice of Hector Santiago.

Elena froze. Hector swooped down and picked her up. He swung her up over his back like a sack of potatoes and walked toward the house.

As she bumped along on Hector's bony shoulder, Elena wondered if she could be dreaming. But, no. It was all happening. Because in the distance, she heard the barking of many dogs. It was a very real sound. She

strained her ears. Was Perro's bark among them?

"Look what the wind blew in," Hector announced, setting Elena down roughly on the floor in the house.

"What the—" The man and woman from the van jumped up so quickly that the table they were sitting at almost fell over.

Scared as she was, Elena couldn't help thinking how funny they looked. Like little kids caught doing something naughty. Now that she saw them up close, she couldn't believe this was really the dognapping ring. These people looked so—well—normal. Like the couple next door or down the block. If you saw them on the street you'd never know. That, Elena decided, was the scariest thing of all.

"Leave her alone." The man, who seemed to be the leader, spoke to Hector sharply. "She's probably just a neighborhood kid. She doesn't know anything."

Would Hector tell all? Elena closed her eyes. He would.

"Neighborhood kid!" Hector laughed a horrible Hector kind of laugh. "Not from this neighborhood! You know who this is? This is one of the kids I was telling you about. The one who put us in touch with the dame. How'd you get here, sister?"

The woman answered for her. "She probably hid in the van."

The dognappers started to yell at each other.

"I thought I told you to lock it!"

"Don't blame me. I got out first!"

"What does she want, anyway?"

Finally Hector said, "The kid thinks we got her dog. She's been rummaging around in the garage. She found these." He held up a handful of dog collars.

Then the screaming really started.

"You mean she owns that mutt you picked up on the River Drive the other day? You dumb creep, grabbing a mongrel. I knew from the beginning that dog was bad news. . . ."

Elena was very confused. Did they have Perro or didn't they?

"So what are we going to do now?" asked the woman.

"Yeah, now it's a mess. They'll be looking for her. You didn't even get the money from the dame. And if we were followed . . ."

"Did you call the cops, little lady?" Hector's voice was full of menace.

Elena didn't answer. *I wish I had called someone*, she thought.

Then Hector sealed her doom. Hector, in his horrible doomsday voice. "There's only one thing we can do," he said. "Get rid of her. Take her and dump her where we dumped the animals. Where no one's gonna look for her."

Now Elena was really, truly terrified. They must have killed some of the dogs. Now they were going to kill her. In her worst nightmares, Elena had never dreamed of anything like this. Mystery or adventure was one thing. But this was a matter of life and death!

A *clue*, thought Elena. *I must leave a clue, in case Michael and the others come. If somehow they should track the dark red van to this house, I've got to leave something to show that I was here.*

Her hand fumbled in the pockets of her yellow jeans. There was nothing there. No. Wait. She felt something. She remembered what it was. *If Michael sees it, he'll know. He'll remember.* Everyone was getting ready to clear out. She had one second. Her hand opened.

She dropped the something on the messy floor of the ramshackle house.

Not a moment too soon. Hector picked her up and stuffed her into a burlap sack head first. He swung her over his shoulder.

Elena felt herself being carried along. She couldn't see where she was going. But she could hear the crunch of sand underfoot. And now she could hear the sound of lapping water coming nearer.

She screamed as loud as she could and tried, from inside the sack, to kick Hector.

Hector only laughed.

It was no use. He was going to drown her!

CHAPTER 9

Clamshell

It was eight o'clock when Michael and Bonnie left the *Taza de Oro*. They were both bitterly disappointed. They had expected to feel better after their meeting with Hector. The least they had expected was a clue about what had happened to Perro and Madame Bovary. As it was, they were no closer to solving the mystery than they had been this morning.

"Listen, kid, I have to leave," Bonnie said. "I'm going to hop a cab. I don't see skating home on all this money at this hour. You two want a lift?"

Michael shook his head. "No thanks," he said. "I'll go over and tell Elena what happened. We'll talk to you tomorrow about our next step."

Michael was trying to pretend there *was* a next step.

Carefully, they avoided looking at each other. If they had, they would have been forced to admit that they might be at the end of the trail. They had no proof, no dogs, and no real clues.

"Sure. Keep in touch," said Bonnie. And she skated to the curb and raised her arm to hail a cab.

Michael crossed the street without looking back. A small nagging worry began to creep up on him. Why hadn't Elena come out of the coffee shop? She must have seen them. She must be dying to know what happened. It wasn't like her to hang back. He had even re-membered her egg rolls. She must have seen the bag he was carrying. How come she hadn't come dashing out for her favorite Chinese food?

It didn't take long to discover why Elena hadn't come out to greet them.

Elena wasn't there.

His heart beating furiously, Michael questioned the waitress in the coffee shop.

"Sure. I remember her. Little skinny dark-haired kid with braids. Nursed a Coke and nibbled at a burger for a long time. She left here about a half hour ago. I think she saw someone she knew. There was a red van outside and . . ."

The van again. First Perro, then Madame Bovary and now Elena. And always the red van kept coming up. . . .

This was a job for the police. But first Michael called home, just in case Elena was there. She wasn't. But Grandma and Mama were. And so was Joe Bowler. Michael lost no time in spilling the whole story. And about time, too, as they all told him on the phone.

"Stay right where you are." It seemed as if Joe Bowler was at the coffee shop almost before Michael hung up the phone.

Joe Bowler was a customs agent and a law enforcement officer. So he knew how to get answers to questions. Michael was glad that Joe and the police would be involved now. A miss-

ing dog was one thing, but a missing sister was another!

Joe asked the questions and Michael answered them.

As they stood outside the coffee shop, Michael told him everything. He told him about Mr. Gold's warning. About Perro and that awful day. About Madame Bovary and the next day. He told about the woman at the Animal Shelter. He told about tracking Hector down at the Alcort Hotel, and about the *Taza de Oro*. About how Hector had come, how he had gone and what he said. He told Joe about Bonnie Balsam, and how they had suspected her at first. And of course he talked about the mysterious dark red van with Jersey plates.

Michael worried that he hadn't told everything in the right order. But Joe kept nodding and making notes.

"How come you left Elena sitting alone out there?"

"We tossed for it." Michael swallowed miserably. "I won."

Joe could see that Michael felt bad about that. He tried to look on the bright side of things.

"It's not likely that the gang picked her up. We don't even know if Hector told them about you and Elena. He might have been double-crossing them. You never know. Even if he did mention his meeting with you, they would have been on the lookout for cops, not for a little girl."

Michael tried to put himself in Elena's place, sitting in a coffee shop, watching.

"Suppose . . . they drive up in a dark red van. . . . Suppose Elena thinks they are going to come into the restaurant to do something to us. Suppose she panics and runs out and . . ."

No. that wasn't Elena. Elena was too smart. She wouldn't have done that. She would have called Joe Bowler if she thought they were in danger. Michael tried a new angle.

"The dark red van shows up. Elena has the chance to look in it close up, maybe even open the back. And she discovers evidence."

Now Joe was getting the idea.

Michael continued. "Now supposing they come back to the van. Elena doesn't have time to get out. She pops into the back. They drive away, and. . . ."

Joe and Michael looked at each other. They both felt sure that they were on the right track. There was only one problem. How do you locate a dark red van with Jersey plates that could have gone *north*, *south*, *east* or *west*?

Joe Bowler groaned. "It'll take us days. It looks like your friend Hector gave us the slip."

Still, Michael refused to give up. "Maybe we should check out the restaurant."

"Good idea!" Joe agreed.

They crossed the street. As soon as they entered the *Taza de Oro* Michael spied the jacket on the hook above the booth where they had been sitting.

99

"Hey! There's Hector's jacket. He left it." Their hands were in the pockets even before they had the jacket off the hook. In no time at all they had found a ratty-looking address book and started thumbing through it.

There weren't that many names and addresses. Hector didn't have many friends. . . .

Joe paused over one entry way in the back. It was under Z, even though it began with C. Clamshell. And it had a little star next to it.

"Maybe it's the name of a motel, or something. Darn! It takes so much time." Joe picked up the phone. He made a call and asked someone to check out all the names of motels in the area to see if there was one called The Clamshell.

"If there is one, it would be at the seashore," he reasoned. In a few minutes the answer came back. No Clamshell Hotels or Motels in this area. Joe's voice showed that he was discouraged.

Now Michael got another idea.

"What if Clamshell isn't a motel? What if

it's a place?" he ventured.

You could tell that Joe Bowler thought Michael's idea was a good one. In about two seconds he was across the street and in his car. He grabbed the map from inside the glove compartment. Joe and Michael ran their fingers up and down the list of towns in neighboring states. Then they started in on their state.

Michael was the one to hit pay dirt. "Here's something. Clamshell Cove. On Sarten's Island. About twenty minutes from here. It could be a coincidence, but. . . ."

"Let's go."

By the time Michael had the map folded they were heading across town to the East Water Drive. They could only hope that they were crossing the same bridge that the van had crossed. After the second bridge, Joe turned on the siren. Then he reached for a two-way radio mike under the dashboard. It was the first time Michael realized that Joe drove an unmarked police car.

101

"Who are you calling?" he yelled, over the
noise of the siren.

"Some friends," Joe yelled back.

It looked like Joe had a lot of friends. Sirens were sounding all over the place. Michael turned around and discovered that he was at the head of a caravan of police cars all heading in the direction of Sarten's Island and Clamshell Cove.

They found Clamshell Cove at about nine-thirty. It was a deserted town. Just a few blocks of ramshackle houses that marked what had once been a thriving fishing village. Driving through the deserted streets, Michael strained his eyes for a glimpse of some kind of life. And then they saw it. At the end of a dead end street was one gray, weather-beaten house with a few lights on. The door was open.

"This is it, all right," said Joe Bowler as they stood in the doorway of the gray house. He pointed to the overturned table and the coffee still steaming on the hot plate. "They must have pulled out of here in a hurry. And not long ago. Look at these." He held up some of the evidence that Elena had found before — dog collars.

As soon as they realized that the dognappers weren't there anymore, Joe sent all but one of the other police cars to search for the dark red van. Two officers searched for clues outside. Meanwhile, he and Michael looked for clues to Elena's whereabouts inside.

"Do you think she was here?" Michael asked Joe.

"I don't know. I can't tell," Joe answered, trying to keep the worry out of his voice. "We'll just have to keep looking."

For the next half hour, they went over every inch of the house. As they went through one room after another, turning up nothing, Michael's lips began to move. He began to talk quietly to himself. *I take back every mean thing I ever said to her. I'll never tease her again. I'll never do anything bad again. If only we could find a sign that she was here. Any old thing will do. Come on,* he pleaded out loud, *give us a break!*

Just then Michael spied a wadded piece of paper on the floor. He unfolded it.

"Joe! You have to see this!" Michael shouted.

It was only a small piece of waxed paper on which was printed *Best Turkish Halvah*. But Michael knew that piece of paper. It was the same one Elena had crumpled up and put in the back pocket of her yellow jeans on the fatal Friday that they had received the warning from Mr. Gold.

Good old Elena. She had put it in her pocket because she didn't like to litter. But she must have deliberately dropped the paper on the floor. And with it she had left a message as clear as if she had written "Elena was Here."

CHAPTER 10
The Fishing Boat

Just then a call came in on the police radio. A squad car had picked up the dark red van. Hector and the two dognappers had been caught!

"Was Elena with them?" was Joe's first question.

No. Elena was not with them. And they wouldn't answer any questions about her, either. Not until they had talked with their lawyers.

"She's got to be around here somewhere," Joe said worriedly.

They began to yell for her. Soon the little tip of island echoed with calls of "Elena." They turned the powerful police searchlights on. The beams poked into every cobwebby corner of the house and the garage. But still there was no sign of Elena.

They began to sweep the shoreline with their lights. The beams lit up the piles of oyster shells, the sandy beach and—suddenly out of the darkness they picked up a fishing trawler. It was anchored about a hundred feet out in the bay.

They might not have given it a second thought—after all, the bay was full of boats. Except that on this one—as the lights played over it—they could hear dogs barking!

"Let's go!" called Joe, running along the shore toward a rowboat that would take them out to the trawler.

It seemed to Michael that he had never taken such a long boat ride in his life.

There were no lights on the trawler. But there was a ladder. They climbed aboard and followed the sound of the dogs. They found them in a little room below the deck. There were about a dozen of them, in a room with no food and no water. A dozen hungry, scared-looking animals. Purebred, beautiful dogs—show dogs, many of them. Probably worth a fortune all together.

Michael spotted Madame Bovary right away. But he knew somehow that he wouldn't find Perro.

He thought about how happy Bonnie Balsam would be. But his thoughts turned quickly back to Elena. Where was Elena? They had been calling her name over the noise of the barking dogs. Why wasn't she calling back to them, directing them to where she was?

Joe flashed his light around the dingy cabin. Over in the corner he spied a burlap sack. As they looked closer they noticed something inside it was moving.

Michael was there in a second, opening the top.

It was Elena. Bound and gagged and acting mad because she was so scared.

"You sure took your time," she sputtered as soon as they got the gag off her.

"Big mouth," Michael said gently. And he hugged his sister, burlap and all.

When they got back to shore, things got pretty hectic. Some more policemen arrived.

The hungry dogs they brought back were barking. The people were all talking at once. Elena talked more than anyone. But as Michael pointed out, Elena had been gagged for a long time.

"She has a lot of talking time to make up!" he said, grinning with happiness because his sister had been found.

A half hour later, Bonnie Balsam arrived. The police had called her to come and identify her dog. As it turned out, Madame Bovary identified Bonnie. When she saw her, the little peach-colored poodle leaped into Bonnie's arms, barking and whining as if she would never stop.

It had been a good night's work, all in all. The criminals had been caught, thanks to Elena and Michael. All the "good guys," including Elena, were safe. Bonnie had her dog back. It was no wonder that it took a while to remember that there was a piece of the puzzle still missing.

Perro.

It hit them all at the same time. The next moment Elena remembered what Hector had said.

She blurted it out, her words tumbling over one another in her hurry to tell it all.

"They don't have Perro. They did steal him but something happened. Hector lied. He was just trying to get more money from us."

Elena stopped for breath. Michael gave a little silent cheer for Perro, wherever he was. Maybe he had managed to escape from Operation Hot Dog.

"The gang will be questioned again tomorrow," Joe Bowler said, an arm around each twin. "Maybe we can get something out of them, like where they last saw him."

But both Elena and Michael knew that while they had solved one mystery, they didn't have a single clue to this one.

"When you think about it," Michael puzzled, "what would Operation Hot Dog want with Perro in the first place?"

Joe Bowler came up with a possible answer.

"Hey," he said gently, "they probably thought at first that Perro was a purebred. They nabbed him, and when they found out he wasn't . . ." He hesitated. Then, "I'll get you another dog. We'll go over to the Shelter tomorrow."

"Don't want to get a dog from the Shelter," said Michael.

Bonnie Balsam came up in time to hear the last part of the conversation.

"I just wanted to say . . . that you kids have earned the five hundred dollars. That's the reward I offered for the return of Madame Bovary. And I sure did get her back, thanks to you. So . . ." she gulped, then tried to smile cheerily, "keep the check. You can buy one heck of a dog for five hundred bucks."

"Don't want one heck of a dog," said Elena tiredly. Her lower lip stuck out the way it always did when she was about to cry. "I want Perro."

Well, listen. You can't always have everything you want. That's what everyone told

Elena and Michael. *Life's like that,* they said. *That's the way it goes,* they told them.

And that could have been the end of the story. But was it? If you think so, you can stop reading right now. But if you have a little faith, a little *heart,* keep on to The Last Word.

CHAPTER 11
The Last Word

When the police questioned them, the gang refused to talk about Perro. All they would say was that they didn't have him anymore. That could mean he had been sold or killed. It could mean he was still alive or that he was dead. It could mean there was hope or there wasn't.

Michael and Elena still waited for the phone to ring. But the days passed. No one called. No one answered the ad they had left in the paper. After two weeks they canceled it.

They still asked around the neighborhood. But after a while people shook their heads even before the twins asked, "Have you seen a little rust-and-white dog?"

It looked like Perro was gone for good.

A month passed.

Then one day Joe Bowler called, sounding very cheerful. "I've got a good idea. How about stopping in at the Animal Shelter tomorrow," he suggested. "Maybe it will perk you guys up."

But it seemed like Michael and Elena didn't want to be perked up.

"I don't want to and that's final." Elena spoke for both of them.

"Okay, suit yourself. But I talked to Shirley Crimmins at the Shelter and she said she has a mystery that she wants to talk to you about."

If there was anything that could get Elena and Michael to go somewhere it was a mystery.

"Maybe we could just go and hear what she has to say. . . ." said Michael. He hated to admit it, but he was curious.

"But no looking at dogs," said Elena. "My heart would bleed too much. . . ." Elena loved that expression.

The following morning two curious children left their house. Elena was wearing a new dress that Grandma had trimmed with lace. Michael was wearing his best "I Love Spanish" T-shirt. Both of them were wearing determined expressions. *If that Ms. Crimmins tried to talk them into a dog. . . .*

The Animal Shelter looked just the same. The twins stood on the steps for a minute, remembering all that had happened since the last time they were here.

There were the cement animals, still scampering across the face of the building. And there was the lobby, still lined with pictures of dogs and cats and birds. And there was Ms. Crimmins, as starchy as ever.

"Well, here you are," she said briskly. "You certainly took your time about it."

Elena was about to say that she hadn't wanted to come at all, but Michael shushed her with a look.

"I don't have all day. I have to go on my rounds. So why don't you walk through with me. We'll talk as we go."

Again Elena started to object. And again Michael signaled her to cool it.

So once again they passed through the corridors. Past the beagle and terrier and shepherd and spaniel dogs. Past the seal point and blue point and calico and angora cats. And past all the combinations of every kind of dog and cat waiting to be adopted.

None of them could take the place of Perro. But they *were* adorable.

"So what I was thinking," said Ms. Crimmins, "was that you could work for us, you know—sort of spread the word. Tell people about the Shelter and what we do here. Maybe you could get some people to adopt animals."

So that's what she wanted to talk to them about. But what was the mystery?

Now the white-coated Ms. Crimmins was standing in front of a closed door.

"I have to go in here now. This is the infirmary. It's where we keep the dogs that are brought to us when they're hurt or sick."

She had her hand on the doorknob.

"Some of them are sicker than others. Sometimes they're just plain starving. Others have gotten hit by cars. . . ."

She hesitated, then pushed her shoulder against the door. She walked into the room, still talking. Elena and Michael followed.

"One little fellow in here was hit by a car. Here, come this way, I'll show him to you. Miracle he wasn't killed. . . . Someone found him and tried to nurse him back to health. They must have kept him for a while but his leg wasn't getting any better. So they brought him to us."

"Is he going to be better?" asked Elena. She was getting more interested in the story.

"Did he have a license?" Michael asked. "Any idea who he belonged to? Did the person who found him leave a name?"

Michael was beginning to collect facts, a sure sign that he was getting interested, too.

Ms. Crimmins laughed. "No. No collar. but I'm sure he's not a stray. That's what I brought you here for. I thought maybe you could help us track down the owner. What he needs now more than anything is a good home."

"Don't you?" she asked the small bundle of fur curled up in the corner of a cage.

The bundle's tail began to wag like an ostrich plume. It was trying to stand up on its three good legs, just as Elena and Michael got their first look at the little dog.

It was Perro.

So there was a happy ending after all, thanks to Joe Bowler, Shirley Crimmins, and some good detective work.

Next day, the reward money from Bonnie came out from under the flan pan and went into the bank. It would be for Elena and Michael's college fund.

Grandma was busy for weeks, telling everyone in the neighborhood about *el milagro*—the miracle.

Meanwhile, Hector Santiago and the two other members of the gang were convicted of stealing and of cruelty to animals. They went off to jail, where they belonged.

Mr. Gold stayed where he was, on the stoop of No. 32, giving out halvah and good advice.

As for Bonnie Balsam, she became a famous recording star and Madame Bovary soared to the top of the charts with her. You can see their pictures on record albums everywhere.

Perro's leg healed perfectly. If you don't believe it, he'll give you his paw so you can check it out.

No more dogs disappeared. Things slowly returned to normal. But of course even on a normal block something unusual happens every once in a while. Elena and Michael know that.

BARBARA BRENNER is the author of more than thirty-five books for young readers, including *Mystery of the Plumed Serpent*, another Capers book from Knopf. *Wagon Wheels* (a 1978 ALA Notable Book), *On the Frontier with Mr. Audubon* ("An Outstanding Book of the Year," *The New York Times*), and *A Snake-Lover's Diary* are among her most well-known titles. Her articles have appeared in *Cricket, Sierra Club*, and many other magazines. *A Killing Season* is her latest novel for older readers.

Ms. Brenner is an associate editor in the publications division of Bank Street College. She and her husband, illustrator Fred Brenner, live in Lords Valley, Pennsylvania.

More Mystery Capers from Knopf!

Man from the Sky, AVI
The Mystery on Bleeker Street, WILLIAM H. HOOKS
The Mystery on Liberty Street, WILLIAM H. HOOKS
Mystery of the Plumed Serpent, BARBARA BRENNER
The Robot and Rebecca:
The Mystery of the Code-Carrying Kids, JANE YOLEN
The Robot and Rebecca and the Missing Owser, JANE YOLEN
The Case of the Weird Street Firebug, CAROL RUSSELL LAW
Who Stole The Wizard of Oz?, AVI

Capers are:

"That rare series of fast-reading, high motivational
books which should be among the 'basics' in our schools.
Students will grab these books off the shelves
in any classroom or library."

—M. JERRY WEISS
Distinguished Service Professor
of Communications Jersey City State College